The story of Cinderella has become one of the most well-known fairy tales. And some people think it's just that—a fairy tale. They refuse to believe that mice and birds could sew a dress or that only one maiden in an entire kingdom could fit into a particular slipper. And they are absolutely positively certain that magic can't be real. But Cinderella's tale is not just some story someone made up. It's all true. Every bit of it happened, just like the story says. I know because I was there.

I'm Cinderella's fairy godmother. And I assure you my magic is very, very real. I'd been watching over my dear Cinderella since she was a child, waiting for the moment when I could swoop into her life with a little Bibbidi! Bobbidi! Boo! Because if anyone deserved a bit of magic, it was Cinderella. I'd never seen such a genuine, kind, and caring child. And she grew into a compassionate, graceful, and elegant young woman that her dear parents would have been incredibly proud of. I still don't know how she managed to turn out as kind-hearted as she is with that vicious, horrible, evil stepmother and those awful stepsisters making her life miserable. I'm just glad I could be there to brighten even one day with a bit of magic.

Being able to play a small part in Cinderella finding her happily ever after is one of my favorite memories—one that I never, ever want to forget. So I've collected little mementos to help me remember all of the special moments leading to Cinderella's dreams coming true.

CINDERELLA

Disney
PRINCESS

CINDERELLA

Princessography

By Molly Hodgin

HARPER FESTIVAL
An Imprint of HarperCollinsPublishers

Once Upon a Time

Once upon a time, in a faraway land, there was a tiny kingdom, peaceful and prosperous, and rich in romance and tradition. Several lovely little French villages lay nestled in the shadow of a shining castle set on a high hill. The king ruled from the castle, watching over the kingdom and doing his best to ensure everyone led contended lives.

A very kind, honorable, and loving young couple lived in the kingdom in a stately château in the country. Good gracious, it was a lovely estate! Their gardens were lush and green, and their château was grand but welcoming. Wide windows filled their home with light, and well-treated servants kept the residence in good repair, the gardens filled with flowers, and the kitchen turning out delicious meals and treats.

The lord and lady of the house were so in love, and so very happy. Their joy was complete when their daughter, Cinderella, was born. The child had eyes as blue as a cloudless sky and hair the color of golden wheat. But their joy would not last. Shortly after Cinderella's birth, her mother passed away. The young lord's heart was heavy, and he missed his wife terribly. But he adored his little girl, and as the years went by, they had a good life. My dear Cinderella loved to sing, and her kindness earned her friendship with all of the animals at the château.

It was her kindness that caught my attention. Anyone sweet and caring enough to befriend mice and birds deserves a little magic in her life!

Of course, Cinderella's father worried about his darling daughter growing up without a mother, so he married a widow, the Lady Tremaine. She was a mother to two daughters of her own, named Drizella and Anastasia. Cinderella was overjoyed and so hoped she and her new sisters would be the best of friends.

At first, it seemed that they might be happy. But Lady Tremaine was a selfish person underneath her cool exterior. She was secretly cruel to the servants, and especially demanding of her husband's time and his money. The château was soon filled with extravagant gifts for her and her daughters. Cinderella's father never forgot to include her as well, but that lovely child would rather have spent time with him than be showered with presents. For soon enough, their time together ran out.

Cinderella's father passed away, leaving his family with no income. It was then that Lady Tremaine showed her true colors. She had always resented Cinderella. Lady Tremaine was jealous over every moment of attention that Cinderella got from her father. Now that Cinderella's father was gone, her stepmother no longer had to pretend to care for the child she had always envied.

Time to Start Another Day

Dear Cinderella spent her days cleaning, cooking, washing, and mending for her stepmother and stepsisters. She was up with the dawn each morning, enjoying the peaceful moments before the castle bells announced that it was time to start her day. After that, it seemed like Cinderella never had a quiet moment without someone shouting, "Cinderella! Cinderella!" and adding another chore to her list.

Why, some days poor Cinderella didn't even have time to feed herself she was so busy working! When Cinderella did have a spare moment, she still had to wash and mend her own threadbare dresses and aprons.

It was a difficult and tiring life, but did Cinderella lose hope? No, she most certainly did not! For with each dawn she found new hope that someday her dreams of happiness would come true. She found beauty in little things and made her own sunshine when the days were darkest. To remind herself to keep dreaming, she even kept a list each day of things she was thankful for or little events that made her happy. She loved the days when her stepsisters had their music lessons. She would listen as she went through her chores and practice her own singing.

A sweet song always helped Cinderella get through the worst of her chores— even scrubbing the marble floors for hours only to discover Lucifer the cat had tracked in mud and she had to scrub them all over again.

Happy Thoughts

We found a new mouse this morning to join our little family. I named him Gus and he's such a sweet little fellow!

A lovely sunny day makes working in the garden and feeding the animals delightful.

Stepmother, Drizella, and Anastasia all slept in today. It was such a relief to have a little more time to get my morning chores done.

Music lessons today! Stepmother's piano playing really is lovely to sing along to.

The strawberries are in season and we all had strawberries with a little cream for dessert—delicious!

Cinderella's Helpers

Cinderella believed every animal was a friend just waiting to make her acquaintance. And most animals, with the exception of one wicked cat, were thrilled to be her friend as well. She made clothes out of scraps for the mice and birds to keep them warm in the drafty château and made sure they always had food to eat, even when there was little to spare.

The Mice

The mice of the château were some of Cinderella's greatest allies. After Cinderella's father died, Lady Tremaine could no longer afford the maintenance to keep the château free of holes and cracks, and mice began to pop up. Lady Tremaine placed traps throughout the house, but they always turned up empty because Cinderella rescued each mouse before Lady Tremaine or Lucifer could find them.

The mice Cinderella saved became her cheerful companions. They lived in the attic with her and brightened even the dreariest days. They helped her with as many of the seemingly endless chores as they could, and in return, she sewed them slippers, dresses, jackets, and even jaunty little caps from scraps of fabric and ribbons.

Jaq

Jaq, short for Jacques, is the leader of the mice. A fearless explorer, he knew the tunnels through that château better than anyone and was always willing to undertake even the most dangerous missions. He loves helping his friends, but his favorite hobby at the château was teasing Lucifer the cat.

Gus

Jaq rescued Gus from a trap, with Cinderella's help, and the two mice became fast friends and partners in crime. Cinderella named him Octavius, Gus for short, but he calls himself Gus-Gus. This little one might have started out timid, but he discovered just how brave he could be while helping his dear new friend, Cinderella. As much as he'd taken to adventure, this gentle mouse's most daring feats often involved sneaking a snack from the kitchen without being caught by that horrible cat.

THE BIRDS

Since Cinderella can sing as sweetly as a bird, it's no surprise that the local bluebirds befriended her. They flew into her room at the château each morning to sing with her, help fluff her pillows, and get her dressed for the day. The birds knew that having a song in your heart helps keep hope alive, so they made sure that Cinderella always had a song to sing.

BRUNO

Bruno the bloodhound is one of Cinderella's oldest friends. The old hound dog had been a part of the household since Cinderella was a little girl and Bruno was just a wiggly little puppy. He may have spent most of his time there dozing on the kitchen floor in front of the fire while dreaming of catching Lucifer, but he was always ready to protect Cinderella if she ever found herself in need.

MAJOR

Major is Cinderella's stallion. He helped Cinderella in the garden and whenever she had to go into the village to run errands for her stepmother and stepsisters. He gladly would have taken Cinderella far away from the château to a better life if his old hooves weren't quite so tired.

LUCIFER

Lucifer is Lady Tremaine's very pampered and very manipulative cat. He had it out for Cinderella, Bruno, and most especially the mice of the château—or the cat-eau as he likes to think of it. This spoiled cat thinks the world revolves around him. He loves getting others in trouble and would never miss a chance to make a mess for Cinderella to clean up or to pretend Bruno had injured or scared him. He'd have loved to catch Jaq or Gus, but he was not as smart as he thought he was, and those mice were far braver and much cleverer.

Prince Charming

As heir to the throne, Prince Charming has spent his whole life learning the importance of duty and the mechanics of ruling a kingdom. He has studied languages, diplomacy, mathematics, literature, history, strategy, dancing, music, and etiquette from the best tutors in the kingdom. He met with the local nobility regularly and was intimately involved in the running of the kingdom by his 16th birthday. He was quite ready to rule the realm whenever it became his time.

Marriage was the only area where Prince Charming had ever rebelled against his father's

wishes. The king wanted grandchildren more than just about anything in the world and he insisted that his son find someone with whom he could start a family. It wasn't that the prince was opposed to being wed; he just hadn't met anyone he wanted to marry. Oh, he'd met every eligible princess, duchess, baroness, and highborn lady from every neighboring kingdom, but none of them made his heart sing. He knew it was probably foolish and overly sentimental, but he wanted to marry someone he loved.

Prince Charming was looking for someone who gave him butterflies in his stomach, someone he wanted to spend each and every day with, someone caring and kind who could also make him laugh. He didn't dare admit any of that to his father, so he found some other reason why each potential match wasn't a fit—but he knew he could only put off finding a wife for so long.

After exhausting all the potential highborn matches from neighboring kingdoms, the king sent his son on diplomatic missions to far-distant kingdoms, hoping one of their princesses might catch his eye. The prince enjoyed traveling and making new connections with other monarchs, but he had not met a potential future bride. By the end of each trip, he was ever so grateful to see the white spires of his own castle rising into the sky as he rode home. The only thing that would make each homecoming better would be if his true love were waiting for him at the gate.

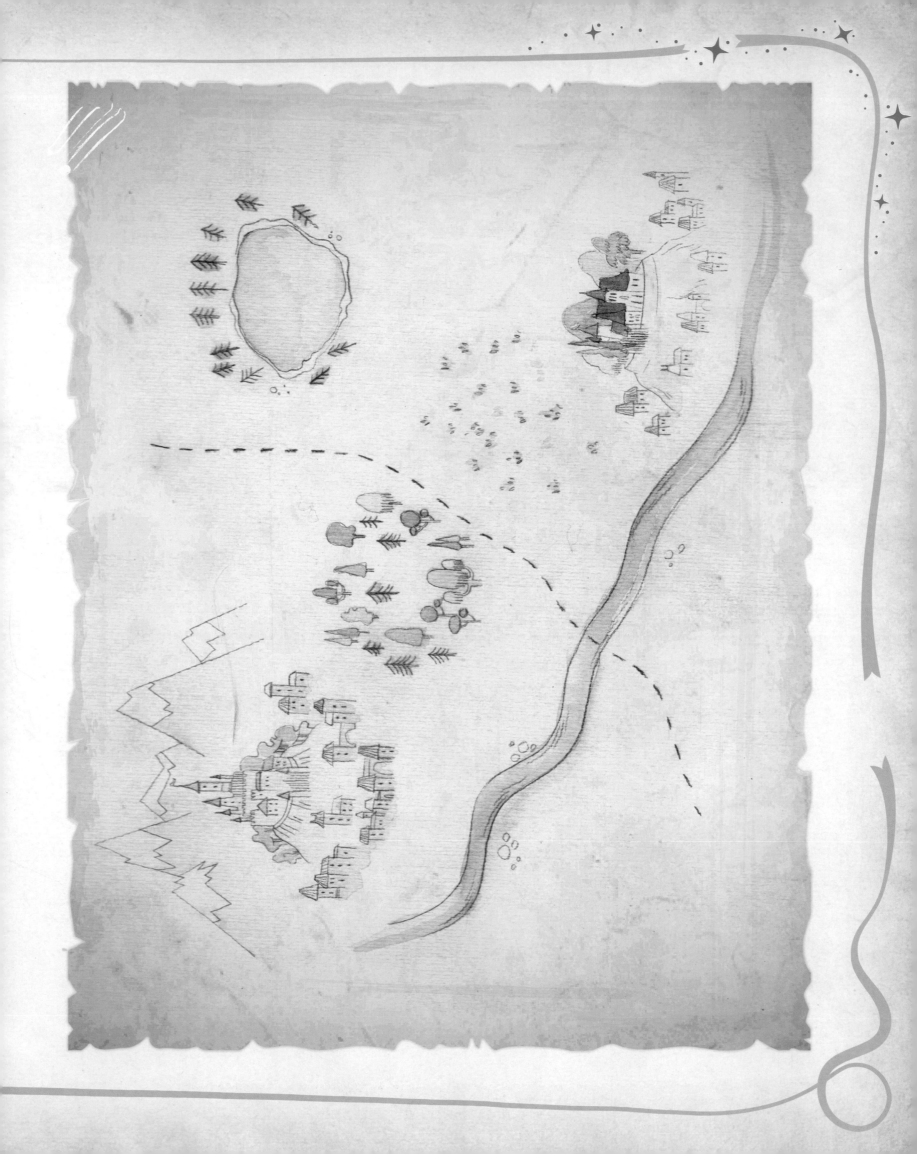

A Royal Invitation

The king was not amused. He had been ruling the kingdom alone for so many years, and he was quite ready to spend his days playing with his future grandchildren. But until his son got married, there wouldn't be any grandchildren. And that made the king exceedingly grumpy.

The king also wanted his son to have a graceful, caring wife to help him through life and the challenges of being responsible for an entire kingdom. So, having exhausted all other options, the king decided to hold a royal ball and invite every eligible maiden in the kingdom.

At that point, it didn't matter to the king if the maidens were highborn or not. He just wanted someone who could rule beside his son, and maybe love the young man a little as well.

Cinderella couldn't believe it when she opened the door and was handed an urgent wax-sealed proclamation from the king. Despite years of desperately trying, Lady Tremaine had never been invited to the palace before. Cinderella knew her

By the
King

An Urgent
Proclamation

stepmother would want to see the proclamation right away, even if it did mean interrupting her stepsisters' music lessons. As suspected, Lady Tremaine was furious at the interruption, but she forgot her anger as soon as she saw the royal envelope. Lady Tremaine ripped it open and read it aloud. When Cinderella heard "By Royal command, every eligible maiden is to attend," her heart practically leapt from her chest. Her stepmother couldn't ignore a royal command. She'd have to let Cinderella attend the ball too. Lady Tremaine promised that Cinderella could go, so long as she finished her chores and found something suitable to wear.

Cinderella raced up to the attic and pulled one of her mother's old gowns from a chest. It was terribly out of style, but the pink cotton fabric was lovely and Cinderella knew that it just needed a few alterations. She'd let out the skirt to make it fuller and add some ruffles and bows—maybe even a bit of lace! Yes, it was perfect. She could just see herself wearing it to dance with the prince.

Helping Hands

Lady Tremaine had no intention of letting beautiful, charming, fresh-faced Cinderella attend the ball alongside her own two daughters. That wicked woman knew just how to get Cinderella's hopes up and then dash them to pieces. The list of chores she'd given Cinderella would easily take the rest of the day. Lady Tremaine continued to add task after task to keep Cinderella too busy to work on her own dress.

Cinderella may not have guessed Lady Tremaine's plan, but the mice and birds knew exactly what was happening. And while Cinderella swept and ironed and cooked and cleaned, they decided to fix her dress for her. The mice cut and stitched the fabric. And the birds helped lift the mice to reach the sleeves and neckline, all while singing a happy tune.

Father,

This kingdom is small, but rich in resources and culture. The king and queen have done a wonderful job of passing laws to protect their subjects and help them develop advantageous trade deals with neighboring kingdoms. We should consider establishing more formal trade agreements for their citrus fruits and fine fabrics. I have never before had such tasty lemons, and their silks are particularly fine. I believe the ladies of our kingdom would very much appreciate the opportunity to purchase such fabrics.

The tour of the kingdom was most illuminating. The king tells me that investing in bridges and roads has been a high priority, and indeed, the carriage rides were quite smooth. Perhaps we should look into more cobblestone roads through our villages? Their fountains and benches are all in good repair, and the whole kingdom gives the impression of affluence and good health. The princess has regaled me with tales of lovely beaches and sea views in the southernmost part of the kingdom. Perhaps I can venture farther south during a future visit.

I met several times with the fair princess. I enjoyed discussing the complexities of running a kingdom with her and exchanging ideas and goals. She has become a very dear friend. But she is not a match for marriage, I'm afraid. I know, Father, you had hoped for a proposal, but my feelings for her are those of deep friendship. I would like to invite her to come and visit our kingdom, as I believe the goodwill between us can blossom into an alliance that would serve us well.

Respectfully Submitted,
Prince Charming

...Jaq scoured the château collecting ...ribbons, beads, and a sash ...Drizella and Anastasia. Those ...d quite a time collecting their ...thout Lucifer catching them, but ...they did. By seven o'clock, when ...arrived to take Lady Tremaine ...ghters to the ball, the animals ...inderella with the finished dress. ...lla looked like a princess in her ...the soft, rose-colored silk bringing ...y cheeks and pink lips and the ...r-colored beads complementing ...yes. As soon as her stepmother and ...s saw her, they knew she would ...hem horribly at the ball. Spotting a ...eir own discarded ribbons and beads ...rella's gown, Anastasia and Drizella— ...rrible girls!—ripped that lovely new ...art. Lady Tremaine and her daughters ...derella standing alone in the front hall ...rags as they hurried off into the night ...d the ball.

Lady Tremaine

The Lady Tremaine is one of the cruelest, most vindictive, and downright wickedest people I've ever come across—and that's saying something; we fairy godmothers have seen our fair share of evildoers. I'd say she was heartless, but I do believe she loves her daughters and Lucifer, at least as much as she's capable of loving anyone. So perhaps instead I can say that her heart is very small indeed. She's a handsome woman, with emerald-green eyes, sharp features, graying hair, and a haughty stare that leaves even her daughters trembling with fear.

Lady Tremaine did not marry Cinderella's father for love. As a widow, she had no other way of providing for herself and her daughters in the luxurious manner to which she was accustomed. Sure, she could have learned a trade and gotten a job, but that would have meant doing actual work— something Lady Tremaine feels is far beneath her.

IF YOU DON'T COUNT HER UGLY PERSONALITY.

Cold, cruel, and bitterly jealous of Cinderella's charm and beauty, Lady Tremaine was grimly determined to advance the interests of her own two awkward daughters, no matter the cost to anyone else. She saw Cinderella as a threat to her daughters' futures right from the start. Lady Tremaine's goal has always been to marry her daughters off to the richest husbands she could find, and she feared that no noble man would even think of marrying Drizella or Anastasia once he got to know the lovely Cinderella. Really, those three poor girls never even had a chance at getting along.

So, Lady Tremaine set out to crush Cinderella's spirit. Cinderella was still just a little girl when her wicked stepmother sold off her family's prized possessions, made her a servant in her own house, and withheld all love and kindness. Cinderella spent so many nights crying herself to sleep, and Lady Tremaine just laughed. And the night of the ball? Lady Tremaine promising that Cinderella could attend, only to snatch that promise away, was so cruel it almost destroyed Cinderella's ability to dream and hope. Of course, the lady's hands were clean. She didn't destroy Cinderella's dress herself; all it took was one expertly placed comment about Cinderella's dress using materials taken from her stepsisters' wardrobes, and Drizella and Anastasia did her dirty work for her.

Perhaps the most dangerous thing about Lady Tremaine is just how smart and devious she is. A clever schemer who takes her time and plans ahead is always scarier to me than someone motivated by passion or revenge. The smart ones almost never make mistakes. Had it not been for me and my magical meddling, Lady Tremaine would likely have kept Cinderella trapped as a servant forever.

Cinderella's Stepsisters

Cinderella tried her best to be friends with her stepsisters, but they insisted on treating her like a servant, not daring to ignore their mother's wishes. Still, Cinderella wanted to keep everyone happy, so she kept a running list of things that her stepsisters liked and things they did not like. She found that the best way to avoid trouble was to know what to look out for.

Drizella

The apple didn't fall far from the tree with Drizella, unfortunately. She looks like her mother, Lady Tremaine, with her dark hair, dark eyes, and tall, thin figure. And she's just as cruel and selfish—but not nearly as clever. Drizella considers herself a great beauty and a talented soprano to boot, although I think people would pay rather large sums of money to avoid hearing her sing. Some would consider her a handsome woman, if it weren't for her beastly attitude and sour disposition.

Despite years of dancing lessons, Drizella is not particularly graceful and is still known to tread on her partner's feet. She favors shades of chartreuse and pale yellow with green or teal accents and prefers to wear long dresses that sweep the ground to conceal her rather large feet. Drizella parts her dark hair down the middle and then pins it back, letting it hang in large curls down her back. Bows and feathers are her favorite hair accessories, and she makes Cinderella iron her ribbons every morning. Drizella desperately wants to attract a rich husband to please her mother and secretly hopes to find a richer husband than her younger sister, proving once and for all that she is her mother's favorite.

Drizella's Likes

The color green

Hair ribbons

Breakfast in bed

Singing

Jewelry

New gowns

Her mother's approval

Drizella's Dislikes

Her large feet

Losing at anything

When her mother favors Anastasia

Toast that is too crisp

When her skirts are not ironed just so

If her mending takes more than a day to complete

Anything dirty or dusty

Not being invited to events

Riding horses

Having to wait

Reading

Writing letters

Wearing out of style dresses

Rain

ANASTASIA

Anastasia is selfish and silly but not nearly as cruel as her mother and older sister. Oh, she still delights in ordering Cinderella around, but mostly because she was raised to be spoiled and wouldn't dare go against her mother's wishes. Anastasia's voice is far too thin for singing, so she attempted to learn to play the flute, but her flute playing is just as off-key as her voice. Why, even Lucifer can't be tricked into listening! Anastasia is not an animal lover. She tolerates Lucifer because she is terrified of mice. She panicked when she found Gus hiding from Lucifer under her teacup one morning and accused Cinderella of putting him there as a vicious practical joke.

Anastasia loves to daydream about marrying a rich lord or duke and moving away from her mother and sister. She loves purple and pink and favors long dresses like her sister. Anastasia knows that her long, shiny auburn hair is her best feature. She has thick bangs in the front and pulls part of her hair up at the crown of her head, where she secures it with a golden clip, letting the rest fall down her back in thick ringlets. Like her sister, Anastasia isn't much of a dancer. Her large feet make her especially prone to tripping. She tried her best to nab Prince Charming for her mother's sake, but no amount of trying could make her foot fit in Cinderella's delicate glass slipper.

Anastasia's Likes

The color pink

Brushing her hair

Cakes

Cookies

Breakfast tea with lots of sugar and cream

Being comfortable

Her mother's approval

Lazing about

Reading

Anastasia's Dislikes

Animals, especially mice

Playing the flute

Her clumsiness

Practicing etiquette

Spending time outdoors

BIBBIDI! BOBBIDI! BOO!

Now, this is the very best part of the story, in my opinion, because this is the part where I come in! As Cinderella ran out to the garden in her ruined dress, tears streaming down her lovely face, I knew that this was the moment I'd been waiting for. I only had one chance to help dear, sweet Cinderella, and this was the perfect time. If I could get her to that ball, she would be free to meet new people and would see that not everyone is as cruel as her stepmother and her stepsisters.

Of course, I hoped she might catch the eye of a young gentleman—or even the prince—but I would have been content with anything that helped her escape the cruel drudgery of her daily life in the château. Even if only for one incredible night.

So, I waved my wand and I materialized in front of Cinderella and her friends in a rush of fairy dust. They were so surprised! But there wasn't a moment to lose, so I set about getting her ready for that ball right away. First, I turned a large pumpkin from the garden into a shining white coach with delicate, vine-inspired filigree and a soft pink-velvet seat inside. Then I turned Jaq, Gus, and two other mice into white horses with gold bridles and tack. Next, Major and Bruno became the carriage's driver and footman. And then Cinderella was ready to go. I was so excited to get her on the road that I almost forgot to get Cinderella herself dressed for the ball! Silly me.

Wand Work
A Primer

Knowing the correct magic words is only the beginning to mastering your fairy godmother magic. It takes more than words to make the magic happen, as it were! Your hand gestures matter every bit as much. There are several rules and guidelines to ensuring your magic functions properly.

1. First you should give your wand a good shake to get the fairy dust flowing. A little tap can sometimes help, too.

2. Point your wand definitively at the item you want to change. Give that wand a firm point. I forgot to do this my first time with a wand and instead of transforming straw into gold, I accidentally transformed the man I was helping into a gold statue. Whoops!

3. Next, move your wand in a loose figure-eight motion a few times as you picture the transformation you want clearly in your mind's eye. Focus, and breathe deeply. I always do three figure eights—no more, no less. I like to wave my other hand a bit for balance while I'm at it.

4. Now give your wand a gentle flick in the direction of the object. A sparkling stream of fairy dust should flow from the tip out to the object you want to transform. A quick flick can change something small, but you've really got to put some muscle into it to turn a pumpkin into a huge carriage!

5. For a particularly complex object, you may need to follow your flick with a spiral motion. Both ball gowns and glass slippers require a spiral.

6. Once the transformation has occurred, tip your wand back up toward the sky to stop the flow of magic.

The Perfect Dress

Cinderella needed to look perfect for the ball. The dress her friends had made her was pretty, but her cruel stepsisters had gone and ruined it. If Cinderella was going to catch everyone's eye, especially the prince's, then she would need to look the part of a princess.

Well, after a few measurements, a swirl of my wand, and a little Bibbidi! Bobbidi! Boo! Cinderella's rags were transformed into a sparkling silvery-blue dress with white satin gloves. Her mussed hair was slicked up in an elegant bun with a shining ribbon holding it in place, and two dazzling glass slippers appeared on her tiny feet. She looked like she was wrapped in starlight, and her eyes glowed with happiness. I'd never seen anyone look lovelier.

My part was done! Cinderella had everything she needed. Now all that was left was to send her on her way to the palace.

How to Conduct a Magical Makeover

Now, as I mentioned before, no fairy godmother can make something out of nothing. Cinderella was, by far, my most stunning makeover. Of course, it helped that Cinderella is so beautiful all by herself, both inside and out. No amount of magic can change the true nature of a person; Cinderella didn't require any spells to make her even more wonderful and caring. She just needed to look the part so she could get inside the castle walls. Her makeover was textbook, really.

First, I measured her with my wand—her skirt needed to be seven wand lengths long. Then I took into account her blue eyes, creamy white skin, and golden hair. Her eyes were red and puffy from crying and her hair a little brittle and dry—so she really did need my help! I pointed my wand and focused, and with a flick and spiral, the transformation began. My magic soothed her puffy eyes and dried her tears. Then it smoothed out her hair, pulling it up in an elegant chignon. Her lips and cheeks were rosy pink, and her skin practically glowed.

In the blink of an eye, I transformed the rags that were left from her pink cotton dress into the lightest of glittery silk spun from the most magical caterpillars in the fairy realm. Their silk is the color of moonlight on the ocean, a silvery blue that I knew would complement Cinderella's eyes perfectly. The gown had a full skirt with layers of lace petticoats and a fitted bodice. It sparkled and shimmered with fairy dust as she moved.

Attention to detail is key when it comes to magical makeovers. Nothing can be overlooked! I made sure she had long silk gloves, perfectly soft for holding hands while dancing, glittering diamond earrings, and a soft black satin ribbon around her neck. I added a touch more silk with a ribbon for her hair.

Her mother's best shoes were lovely, but they didn't match the new gown I was whipping up for her. Besides, I had something more unique in mind. I transformed them into sparkling glass slippers with low heels and an elegant design. Not every fairy godmother could have created something quite so perfect, but if I do say so myself, I'm one of the best!

Now Cinderella was fit for the ball. I dare anyone to turn her away at the door. But to truly shine at the castle and have a night she could remember was entirely up to Cinderella. Magic couldn't help her there. I had no doubt that lovely young woman would make the most of her one evening of freedom.

An Enchanting Evening

The royal ball began at seven o'clock in the evening with the arrival of guest after guest at the palace gates. Elegant coaches followed fine carriages up the cobblestone street to let each guest out at the bottom of the red-carpeted stairs leading up to the castle. Once everyone was seated, dinner was served. Waiters in crisp white uniforms brought out dishes of tender spring peas and carrots, tureens of soup, baskets of warm, buttery bread, and platters of mouthwatering ham and baked pheasant with glasses of crisp, fruity punch.

When it was time for the dancing to begin, each eligible maiden lined up to be presented to the prince. Prince Charming stood on a dais in front of the throne, looking charming indeed in his crimson trousers and ivory jacket with gold trim and epaulettes, as his dark hair shone in the candlelight. He sighed wearily, fidgeting a bit, as each maiden stepped forward and curtsied to him. It had been a long journey back to the palace, and all he wanted was rest, not to meet and greet and dance. Many of the women were beautiful and accomplished, from good families, but none of them could hold a candle to his longing for sleep. That is, until he saw Cinderella across the room.

Prince Charming had never seen anyone as poised and beautiful as the girl standing at the top of the stairs in the shimmering silvery-blue gown. Her dazzling smile filled his stomach with butterflies. He raced across the room, leaving a line of stunned maidens in his wake, and asked Cinderella to dance.

Cinderella and Prince Charming walked down into the garden and then swept across the terrace, dancing to the soft music and chatting a little. He felt, for the first time, the stirrings of love as he danced with Cinderella. He didn't even know her name, but as they danced he saw that she was kind, considerate, graceful, and interested in *him*, not his title.

But then, the midnight bells began to ring, and his dance partner excused herself so quickly that they didn't even have time for a proper introduction. She left without even realizing she had danced with the prince. Before he could stop her, she was gone. It was like he'd been abruptly woken from a wonderful dream, and he was devastated. He had no idea who his mystery girl was or where she was from. How was he ever going to find her?

ROYAL BALL ETIQUETTE

Guests attending a royal ball must be well dressed, poised, elegant on the dance floor, and most of all, polite. There are two parts to a royal ball: the formal dinner and the dancing that comes afterward. Not all guests are invited to dine with the king, but everyone who receives an invitation should know what is expected of them at all times. Certain rules and forms of etiquette must be followed at a royal event.

Special Guests of the King

3. It is customary to toast to the health of the king and the prosperity of the kingdom at least once during the meal.

4. At the end of the dinner, the king is first to stand and the guests then follow the royal family to the ballroom.

5. No guest may enter the ballroom until properly announced by the herald. Then you may step forward to be presented to the king or prince.

6. When greeting a member of the royal family, it is respectful for gentlemen to bow and ladies to curtsy. The deeper the bow or curtsy, the more respectful it is. A formal bow requires that a gentleman bend forward from the waist so that his upper body is parallel to the floor and hold in that position for at least three seconds. A proper curtsy requires that the lady step back with her left foot and then bend both knees as she leans forward slightly, tipping her head down as well. Her skirts should pool on the floor. She should hold in this position for at least three seconds.

7. Gentlemen ask ladies to dance. Each dance begins with a bow from the gentleman and a curtsy from the lady.

1. Always wait for the king to be seated before you sit.

2. At dinner, no one should eat until the king has taken his first bite.

8. It is customary not to leave the ball until the royal family retires for the evening.

ALTHOUGH, THIS RULE IS CHANGING IN MORE
MODERN KINGDOMS, AND IT'S ABOUT TIME.

Midnight!

Not everyone understands fairy magic. Of course, very few people actually experience fairy magic for themselves, so this is to be expected. But one of the most important things to know is that there are rules to fairy magic—oh yes, even fairy godmothers have to follow rules—and we can never ever change them, no matter how much we wish that we could. Not even to help someone as lovely and deserving as dear Cinderella.

YOU CAN'T MAKE SOMETHING OUT OF NOTHING. Fairy godmothers need *something* to work with—we can't just conjure things out of thin air—which is why Cinderella's coach was made out of a pumpkin.

WE CAN ONLY HELP THOSE WHO TRULY DESERVE IT. Dear, sweet Cinderella never gave up on her dreams, no matter how difficult her situation became. And she was always kind, even to her stepmother and stepsisters, who had hurt her the most and treated her woefully unfairly. Those who are cruel, unkind, or focused on revenge can never be helped by fairy magic.

THERE IS ONLY SO MUCH MAGIC CAN DO. We fairy godmothers do our best, but we are limited.

- We can't make people fall in love.
- We can't do harm to anyone (and we wouldn't even if we could!).
- We can't give anyone money or power.
- We can't help anyone enact revenge.

LUCKILY CINDERELLA DIDN'T NEED ANYTHING NEARLY SO GRANDIOSE!

ALL MAGIC HAS A TIME LIMIT. All fairy godmother spells break at midnight. We can't offer even an extra second of magic, much as we might wish to. I would have loved to give Cinderella a few more minutes at the ball, but there was nothing I could do, *nothing at all*. As soon as the clock struck midnight, Cinderella's dress returned to rags, her coach became a pumpkin, and her horses, footman, and coachman were animals once more.

THERE IS *ALWAYS* AN EXCEPTION TO THE RULES! I might not have been able to give Cinderella any more time at the ball, but I couldn't leave her with nothing after such a promising evening. I was able to sneak in an extra burst of magic to make her glass slippers real. The slippers were already so delicate that it only took the tiniest bit of magic, barely enough to even count! So as Cinderella ran down the palace steps, stepping right out of one slipper and leaving it behind for the grand duke to find, I breathed a big sigh of relief hoping the prince could come up with a way to use it to meet her again.

SOMETIMES WE CAN BEND THE RULES. JUST A SMIDGE.

A Dream Is a Wish Your Heart Makes

I guess I forgot about everything, even the time, but it was so wonderful.
And he was so handsome, and when we danced . . . oh, I'm sure that even
the Prince himself couldn't have been more . . . perfect.

—Cinderella

Cinderella barely made it down the palace steps, into her coach, and down the road to the safety of the forest before the midnight bells finished chiming and all of my magic disappeared in a shower of fairy dust. She found herself standing on the road in her ragged dress with Major, Bruno, four mice, and a smashed pumpkin. There was one lone reminder of her perfect evening—a single glass slipper. Cinderella had a special keepsake to remind her of the ball for the rest of her life. It wasn't all that I'd hoped she would take from the evening, but it was something. And it also held the promise of something more.

Cinderella thought about her dance partner the whole way home. She wondered who he was and what he did each day, and if he was thinking of her too. She would give anything to see him again, even though she knew that it was unlikely.

As soon as she got home, Cinderella raced up to her room and hid the slipper in the back of her wardrobe. She couldn't risk her stepmother finding it, but she wanted to be able to look at it whenever she desired and remember how it felt to have a dream come true. She danced around her room, humming the music she'd danced to that night, and she resolved that even if she never saw her dance partner again, she was going to find a way to get herself out of her horrible château. She'd hung on for so long, wanting to stay in her family home and hoping that maybe her stepmother would love her, but no longer. Market day was next week, so Cinderella decided she'd patch up her best dress and look for other employment when she went to town to buy meat, flour, fabric, and thread for the household. Surely there must be another, kinder family in town in need of a maid or seamstress.

With that in mind, Cinderella fell fast asleep and dreamed about dancing with the handsome stranger all night long.

The Search for the Glass Slipper

Prince Charming was devastated when Cinderella disappeared from the ball before he could learn her name, leaving behind nothing but a delicate glass slipper. He knew, beyond a shadow of a doubt, that his mystery girl was the only girl he'd met that he would even consider marrying.

The king wasn't about to let Cinderella get away—oh no!—not when his son had finally found someone he wanted to marry. So, he sent the grand duke out with a proclamation and a map. The grand duke was to try the glass slipper on the foot of every maiden in the kingdom. No one was to be skipped, no matter her position. He was going to leave no stone—or maiden—unturned in his quest to find his son's true love.

The grand duke marched from home to home, fending off hopeful maidens and their overzealous parents, and watching helplessly as girl after girl failed to fit into the glass slipper. He was beginning to think that the girl the prince danced with had been a figment of the young man's imagination when he finally reached the château of Lady Tremaine. He got there not long after that wicked woman locked Cinderella away in her room to keep her far away from the grand duke and the promise of freedom.

WHAT I WOULD HAVE PAID TO SEE LADY TREMAINE'S FACE WHEN CINDERELLA WAS SWEPT OFF TO THE CASTLE TO MARRY THE PRINCE. NOT ONLY DID SHE LOSE HER LONE SERVANT, BUT CINDERELLA WOULD HAVE THE CHANCE TO LIVE OUT THE DREAM THE WOMAN HAD FOR HER OWN DAUGHTERS. SERVES HER RIGHT, THE OLD MEANIE!

Drizella and Anastasia fought valiantly to squeeze their long feet into the tiny slipper. I must give those girls credit for their persistence, but it was no use. I must also thank them because the grand duke would have left much sooner if they'd given up too easily! For while the girls tried on the slipper, Gus and Jaq successfully stole the key to Cinderella's attic room from Lady Tremaine's pocket, outwitted Lucifer, and freed Cinderella.

Dear sweet Cinderella rushed downstairs, to the grand duke's surprise and delight, as she was obviously *much* more pleasant a person than her family. But Lady Tremaine tripped the footman, and the slipper flew through the air and shattered on the marble floor. It seemed that all hope was lost, but then Cinderella produced the other slipper from her apron pocket and slipped it on her foot, proving that she was the prince's mystery girl.

A Royal Wedding

Goodness me! This is my favorite part of the story—the happily ever after. Once the grand duke found Cinderella, he whisked her off to the castle, where Prince Charming proposed immediately, and Cinderella said yes. They spent some time getting to know each other better while the entire castle prepared for them to be wed. The king was so excited that he personally took part in every detail of the wedding planning along with his son and the bride-to-be.

Cinderella and Prince Charming were married on a perfect June morning. I, of course, was there to witness the happy occasion. The morning wedding was the king's idea—he wasn't taking any chances that his lovely daughter-in-law to be might disappear with a puff of magic at midnight!

My heart swelled with pride over having helped make it happen as I watched Cinderella walk down the aisle in a sparkling white gown with a full skirt and elegant long sleeves. She looked so very happy, holding the hand of her new husband, her veil held up by her bird friends. Jaq, Gus, and all of the mice threw rice after the happy couple as they left the church.

As they ran down the stairs to the waiting carriage, Cinderella stepped right out of her shoe, a lovely new glass slipper, courtesy of me (of course!). But this time, the king himself raced down the stairs and helped her back into her slipper. She kissed her new father-in-law's head with all the love of family. Cinderella finally had the happy ending she had always deserved. It was then and there that I knew she'd never need me again.

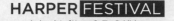

HARPER FESTIVAL
An Imprint of HarperCollinsPublishers

For information address HarperCollins Children's Books, a division of
HarperCollins Publishers, 195 Broadway, New York, NY 10007.
www.harpercollins.com

ISBN 9780062862204

Produced by

INSIGHT KIDS

An Imprint of Insight Editions
PO Box 3088
San Rafael, CA 94912
www.insighteditions.com

© 2018 DISNEY

Publisher: Raoul Goff
Associate Publisher: Vanessa Lopez
Creative Director: Chrissy Kwasnik
Senior Editor: Paul Ruditis
Editorial Assistant: Kaia Waller
Production Editor: Lauren LePera
Production Manager: Greg Steffen

Illustrations by Rafael Mayani, Nicola Lacovetti, and Isabella Grott

Insight Editions would like to thank Stuart Smith, Malea Clark-Nicholson
and Yousef Ghorbani for their design contributions.

Manufactured in China by Insight Editions

18 19 20 21 22 HH 10 9 8 7 6 5 4 3 2 1